ICONS

COLORS

SIGNS

TASCHEN

HONG KONG KÖLN LONDON LOS ANGELES MADRID PARIS TOKYO

Contents
Inhalt
Sommaire

111
Miscellaneous
Verschiedenes
En vrac

123
Danger
Gefahr
Danger

147
Toilets
Toiletten
Toilettes

161
No!
Nein!
Non!

179
Work
Arbeit
Travail

188
Page/Country/
Photographer
Page/Pays/Photographe
Seite/Land/Fotograf

The Ancient Romans used road signs to show the distance to Rome from the different parts of their empire. And until the twentieth century signs didn't really change: They just pointed the way and showed you how far to go. Then cars arrived, speeds went up and suddenly signs were essential for everyone's safety. Drivers had to know where to go, what dangers lay ahead, what other road users were going to do—and they had to know quickly and simply. So circles, triangles, rectangles and octagons decorated with symbols began to sprout up. When cars spread around the world road signs became the only truly international language, created so that anyone from anywhere could understand. While even country-specific signs (you don't see many "koala bear crossing" signs in Norway) are generally easy to understand, that doesn't mean that you won't sometimes need some help. We'd like to think of this book as a road signs language guide, preparation for the next time you hit the road. By the time you've finished reading, you'll know exactly how to read any dangers you might face, whether it's a kangaroo or a landmine.

An den alten Römerstraßen gaben Meilensteine die Entfernung zur Hauptstadt des Imperiums an. Und an diesem Prinzip änderte sich bis zum 20. Jahrhundert nichts: Wegweiser beschränkten sich darauf, Richtung und Entfernung anzuzeigen. Dann kam mit dem Auto die Geschwindigkeit, und Schilder wurden für die Sicherheit der Verkehrsteilnehmer unverzichtbar. Autofahrer brauchten möglichst schnell verständliche Informationen über die Richtung, in die sie fuhren, eventuelle Gefahren und die Absichten der anderen Verkehrsteilnehmer. Bald waren die Straßen mit kreisförmigen, drei-, vier- und achteckigen Schildern mit Symbolen übersät. Verkehrszeichen wurden mit der Verbreitung von Autos auf der ganzen Welt zur allgemeinverständlichen künstlichen Sprache. Selbst wenn sogar landesspezifische Zeichen (in Norwegen sind Schilder, die vor die Straße überquerenden Koalas warnen, eher selten) im Normalfall begreiflich sind, kann man dennoch manchmal Hilfe gebrauchen. Dieses Buch soll auf der nächsten Reise als Wörterbuch für Schilder dienen. Der aufmerksame Leser und Betrachter wird am Ende des Buches genau wissen, ob die Gefahr auf der Straße von einem Känguru oder einer Landmine droht.

Les Romains utilisaient déjà des panneaux de signalisation pour indiquer la distance à laquelle se trouvait Rome des différents points de leur empire. Au reste, de l'Antiquité au 20ᵉ siècle, bien peu de choses changèrent en matière de signalisation : les poteaux indicateurs se contentaient de pointer dans une direction et d'indiquer la distance à parcourir. Puis les automobiles déboulèrent dans le paysage, prirent de la vitesse et, soudain, les panneaux devinrent essentiels à la sécurité de chacun. Les conducteurs devaient non seulement savoir où aller, mais aussi être informés des dangers qui les attendaient, de ce qu'allaient faire les autres usagers de la route, le tout de façon claire et rapide. C'est ainsi que cercles, triangles, rectangles et octogones décorés de symboles commencèrent à pousser et se multiplier sur les routes. Lorsque la voiture se répandit dans le monde, les panneaux suivirent, à tel point qu'ils représentent aujourd'hui le seul langage réellement international, conçu pour être compris par n'importe quel individu en n'importe quel lieu. Cependant, il existe quelques panneaux spécifiques à tel ou tel pays (on ne croise guère de panneau «attention, traversée de koalas» en Norvège) et, s'ils sont en général faciles à déchiffrer, il n'est pas exclu que vous ayez parfois besoin d'aide. Notre ambition a été de faire de ce livre un guide du langage de la signalétique routière, pour vous permettre de réviser en prévision de votre prochaine escapade. Lisez-le jusqu'au bout, et aucun danger de la route ne vous prendra plus au dépourvu, ni kangourou ni mine antipersonnel – pour peu, bien sûr, qu'ils soient signalés.

7
Animals
Tiere
Animaux

Roadkill
Plattgefahren
Accidentés de la route

You are a tortoise based in, say, southern Lithuania. All year long, you've been looking forward to the mating season. Your species has been returning to the same breeding grounds for the last 50,000 years, so it's sort of a tradition. As you set out this year, however, you run into an unexpected obstacle—a brand new highway. You've never crossed one before, and you're a little apprehensive. What should you do? Before you decide to cross the road, here are some statistics you should know. US highways kill six times more deer each year than hunters do. In the UK, some 100,000 rabbits, 100,000 hedgehogs, 47,000 badgers and 5,000 barn owls become road casualties annually, and an estimated 30 percent of the amphibian population (including over a million toads) is flattened.

These figures might sound a little discouraging, but before you turn around and go home, there's another argument to consider. The mating season is very important for you tortoises. A disrupted reproductive cycle can lead a species toward extinction. And with an estimated 20,000 species going extinct each year, your fellow tortoises are counting on you. So maybe it's best to cross the road and take your chances. After all, highways are now a permanent feature of the landscape. There are over 22 million kilometers of road on the planet (enough to stretch to the moon and back 28 times), and more are built every day. Today's highways may even be influencing animal evolution. According to some sources, a new generation of British hedgehogs is genetically disposed to flee from oncoming cars, rather than just curling up in a ball (the traditional hedgehog response). In Venezuela, green iguanas have even integrated the highway into their mating rites: When rival males fight for a mate, the loser must cross the road and start a new life on the other side.

So never mind that tortoises have been around for 200 million years. Highways are here for good. If your species intends to survive, you'll just have to learn to look both ways before you cross.

Stell dir vor, du bist eine Schildkröte in Südlitauen und freust dich schon das ganze Jahr über auf die Paarungszeit. Deine Spezies kehrt seit 50 000 Jahren immer wieder an dieselbe Brutstätte zurück, die Reise dorthin hat also Tradition. In diesem Jahr jedoch stößt du auf ein unerwartes Hindernis – eine neue Autobahn. Da du noch nie eine überquert hast, bist du ein bisschen ängstlich. Was tun?

Bevor du dich anschickst, sie zu überqueren, solltest du dich mit einigen Statistiken vertraut machen. In den USA sterben in jedem Jahr sechsmal mehr Rehe auf den Autobahnen als durch die Kugeln von Jägern. In Großbritannien sind jährlich 100 000 Kaninchen, 100 000 Igel, 47 000 Dachse und 5000 Schleiereulen als Verkehrsopfer zu beklagen, ganz zu schweigen von schätzungsweise 30% aller Amphibien – darunter über 1 Million Kröten –, die platt gefahren werden.

Das klingt nicht gerade ermutigend, aber bevor du umdrehst und dich auf den Heimweg machst, solltest du Folgendes bedenken: Die Paarungszeit ist für euch Schildkröten von größter Bedeutung. Ein unterbrochener Fortpflanzungszyklus kann das Aussterben einer Spezies nach sich ziehen. Da Schätzungen zufolge Jahr für Jahr etwa 20 000 Arten aussterben, zählen deine Mitschildkröten auf dich. Deshalb solltest du vielleicht doch die Straße überqueren und es einfach mal drauf ankommen lassen. Autobahnen gehören heute eben zur Landschaft. Unseren Plane-

ten umspannen Straßen von 22 Millionen km Länge (das ist 28-mal die Strecke von der Erde bis zum Mond und zurück), und die Erde wird kräftig weiter zugepflastert. Autobahnen werden für Tiere mitunter sogar zum Evolutionsfaktor. Es heißt, britische Igel sollen inzwischen genetisch so disponiert sein, dass sie vor herannahenden Fahrzeugen die Flucht ergreifen anstatt sich – wie es der traditionellen Verhaltensweise entspräche – einzuigeln. Die Grünen Leguane in Venezuela haben Autobahnen bereits in ihre Paarungsriten aufgenommen: Wenn rivalisierende Männchen um ein Weibchen kämpfen, muss der Verlierer die Straße überqueren und sich auf der anderen Seite ein neues Leben aufbauen. Also Schluss mit dem Argument, dass Schildkröten schon seit 200 Millionen Jahren existieren. Mit den Autobahnen werdet ihr euch abfinden müssen. Wenn ihr als Spezies überleben wollt, müsst ihr lernen, nach links und rechts zu schauen, bevor ihr die Straße überquert.

Vous êtes une tortue originaire, disons, de Lituanie méridionale. Toute l'année, vous avez attendu avec impatience la saison des amours. Depuis 50000 ans, vos congénères retournent sans faillir sur les mêmes lieux pour s'accoupler. Une tradition, si l'on peut dire. Vous vous mettez donc en route, cette année encore, et voilà que, soudain, vous vous heurtez à un obstacle inattendu : une autoroute flambant neuve. Une première pour vous et vous ressentez une certaine appréhension. Comment faire ?

Avant d'entreprendre la grande traversée, voici quelques statistiques qu'il vaut mieux connaître. Chaque année, les autoroutes américaines tuent six fois plus de cerfs que les chasseurs. Au Royaume-Uni, quelque 100000 lapins, 100000 hérissons, 47000 blaireaux et 5000 chouettes sont victimes d'accidents de la route. Selon les estimations, 30 % des amphibiens (dont plus de un million de crapauds) finiraient en galette sur le bitume.

Bien sûr, ces données ont de quoi vous décourager mais, avant de rebrousser chemin, il est un autre argument à prendre en considération. Vous autres tortues n'ignorez pas l'importance de la saison des amours. Que les cycles de reproduction s'interrompent et c'est l'extinction. Sachant que 20000 espèces (si l'on en croit les estimations) disparaissent chaque année, imaginez à quel point vos congénères comptent sur vous.

Tout compte fait, mieux vaut peut-être tenter le tout pour le tout. En fin de compte, les autoroutes font désormais partie du paysage. À l'heure actuelle, plus de 22 millions de km de routes sillonnent la planète (de quoi couvrir 28 allers-retours entre la Terre et la Lune), et il s'en construit un peu plus chaque jour. Au reste, il est même possible que l'autoroute moderne ait une influence sur l'évolution des espèces animales. Il semblerait ainsi qu'une nouvelle génération de hérissons ait fait son apparition au Royaume-Uni, génétiquement prédisposée à fuir devant une voiture au lieu de se rouler en boule (ce qui est la réaction habituelle de ces animaux). Les iguanes verts du Venezuela ont même intégré l'autoroute dans leurs rituels amoureux : quand des mâles rivaux se disputent une femelle, le perdant est contraint de traverser la route et de refaire sa vie de l'autre côté.

Peu importe donc que les tortues aient été là les premières, qu'elles existent depuis quelque 200 millions d'années – désormais, autant s'y faire : les autoroutes sont là pour longtemps. Si votre espèce a l'intention de survivre, il lui faudra apprendre à regarder à droite et à gauche avant de traverser.

TURTLES CAN BITE
PLEASE DO NOT TOUCH THEM

CAUTION
WATER DRAGON HABITAT

BEWARE

ATTACKING
BIRDS

REDUCE SPEED
AHEAD

WILDLIFE CROSSING

THANK YOU

IMA BEZIHAMBEL

"GAWUL'...INGWENYA"

Don't feed the seagulls
They become aggressive
and will steal food.

PRECAUCION

REDUZCA VELOCIDAD

19

CT AREA

WILDLIFE

LING US

Cranbrook & District
Traffic Safety Commitee

ways

23
Man
Mann
Homme

Walk where
Wohin des Weges?
Marche à l'ombre

It all began with the threat of violence, or so it's thought. The side of the road on which we drive on depends on the side of the body our ancestors carried their swords. When people started moving around, in the days when roads were plagued by footpads and bandits, it paid to walk along the side of the road you could defend yourself best on. So a right-handed man (there probably weren't many women carrying swords and traveling alone) preferred to stay on the left, the better to reach over to his scabbard—carried on the left side of the body—with his right hand. Though if you were leading a cart, it was customary to sit towards the inside of the road, and thus drive on the right. (If you were leading a cart and carrying a sword, you were probably very confused.) Napoleon decreed that people drive on the right, though not all his conquered countries obeyed. Which might explain the current state of affairs—163 countries drive on the right, and 58 on the left. Those numbers aren't necessarily permanent though. Just look at Sweden, which decided in 1967 to change sides to conform with the rest of continental Europe, even though 12 years earlier 82.9

percent of the population had said it was happy on the left. The changeover took a week, and much careful coaching, but there were no fatalities. Elsewhere there are still which-side-of-the-road blackspots between bordering countries: Try driving between Pakistan and China, Thailand and Laos, Namibia and Angola, or arriving in Europe from the British Isles. But just as when there were only carts and swords, it's not really which side of the road you're driving on that poses the real danger, it's the people driving: Every year, more than 1.2 million people are killed on the world's roads.

Alles begann mit der Androhung von Gewalt, so wird jedenfalls behauptet. Auf welcher Straßenseite wir heute fahren, hängt davon ab, auf welcher Körperseite unsere Vorfahren ihre Schwerter trugen. Zu Zeiten, als noch Wegelagerer und Raubritter die Straßen unsicher machten, gingen die Menschen auf der Seite, auf der sie sich besser verteidigen konnten. Deshalb bevorzugte ein rechtshändiger Mann (Frauen waren selten allein unterwegs und trugen noch seltener Schwerter) die linke Straßenseite, da er so besser mit der rechten Hand sein Schwert

aus der links hängenden Scheide ziehen konnte. Wer den Weg allerdings auf einem Karren zurücklegte, saß auf der der Straßenmitte zugewandten Seite und fuhr folglich rechts (für karrenfahrende Schwertträger war das vermutlich äußerst verwirrend). Unter Napoleon war das Rechtsfahren per Verordnung vorgeschrieben, doch nicht alle Länder, die er erobert hatte, hielten sich daran. Darin mag eine Ursache für den heutigen Stand der Dinge liegen: In 163 Ländern herrscht Rechtsverkehr, 58 fahren links – was nicht bedeutet, dass es so bleiben muss. Schweden zum Beispiel beschloss 1967, sich an das übrige Kontinentaleuropa anzupassen und den Rechtsverkehr einzuführen, obwohl sich zwölf Jahre vorher 82,9% der Schweden dafür ausgesprochen hatten, das Linksfahren beizubehalten. Der Wechsel wurde binnen einer Woche vollzogen und verlief dank vorsichtigen Fahrens ohne Todesopfer. Anderswo bilden die Grenzgebiete zwischen rechts und links fahrenden Ländern echte Gefahrenstellen. Das gilt für Fahrten von Pakistan nach China, von Thailand nach Laos, von Namibia nach Angola oder für die Rückkehr auf das europäische Festland nach einem Aufenthalt in Großbritannien.

Aber wie bei Karren und Schwertern besteht die Gefahr nicht so sehr darin, auf welcher Seite der Straße man sich fortbewegt, sondern darin, wer einem entgegenkommt: Jährlich sterben weltweit über 1,2 Millionen Menschen im Straßenverkehr.

Tout a commencé, croit-on, dans la violence et la peur. Le côté de la route où nous conduisons dépend en effet du côté où nos ancêtres portaient leur épée. Lorsque l'on commença à voyager, à une époque où les routes étaient infestées de camelots détrousseurs et autres voleurs de grand chemin, il était recommandé de marcher du côté de la chaussée où l'on était le mieux à même de se défendre. Aussi un droitier (on comptait sans doute bien peu de droitières circulant seules sur les chemins, l'épée au

côté) préférait-il rester du côté gauche, afin de mettre plus facilement la main droite au fourreau, qu'on portait alors sur le côté gauche. Si, en revanche, on conduisait un char ou une carriole, on avait coutume de s'asseoir non côté talus, mais côté route, et par conséquent, de rouler à droite. (Pour peu qu'on conduise un chariot tout en portant l'épée, il y avait de quoi y perdre son latin.) Napoléon décréta que l'on roulerait à droite, ce qui ne veut pas dire que tous les pays conquis par ses soins obtempérèrent. Voilà qui explique peut-être la cacophonie actuelle : on compte dans le monde 163 pays où l'on roule à droite, contre 58 où l'on roule à gauche – chiffres qui ne sont en rien immuables. Citons par exemple la Suède, qui résolut en 1967 de changer le côté de la circulation alors même que, douze

ans plus tôt, 82,9 % de la population s'était déclarée satisfaite de rouler à gauche. La mise en place du nouveau système prit une semaine et nécessita un entraînement soigneusement orchestré, mais il n'y eut pas de victimes. Ailleurs, la confusion règne pour les pays frontaliers où l'on roule ici à gauche et là à droite. Tenez, essayez donc de passer en voiture du Pakistan en Chine, de la Thaïlande au Laos, de Namibie en Angola ou de pénétrer en Europe continentale depuis les Îles britanniques. Cependant, il est une chose qui n'a guère changé depuis le temps des carrioles et des rapières. Comme alors, le danger ne réside pas tant dans le côté de circulation que chez les conducteurs eux-mêmes. Rappellerons-nous que la route fait chaque année plus de 1,2 millions de morts ?

33

9h30 – 10h30
LUNDI
JEUDI
1 MARS AU 1 DEC.

ARRÊT

35
Stop
Halt
Arrêt

Octagon
Oktogon
Octogone

Making its debut in the US in 1915, the STOP sign is now the only official road sign internationally designated to have an octagonal shape. The sign is one of a kind for more than safety reasons—the shape means it requires more cutting (and thus wastage) than the more common squares, triangles and circles. The shape may have been decided on quickly, but getting the final design right took a little longer. At first it featured black letters on a white background, then quickly changed to black on yellow, then red on yellow, before eventually becoming the celebrated white on red. In the USA, it now has "cat's-eye" reflectors, a standard size of 76.2cm by 76.2cm and should be mounted at the height of 2.1m. It's now seen all over the world. While the signs in Spanish-speaking countries in Central and South America still have the Spanish "PARE" or "ALTO," Spain itself uses the English STOP. It wasn't the country's choice though—it was just complying with European Union regulations.

Seit es 1915 in den USA offiziell eingeführt wurde, ist das Stoppschild das einzige offizielle, inter-national anerkannte Verkehrs-zeichen mit acht Ecken. Das Schild ist nicht nur aus Sicher-heitsgründen einzigartig: Wegen seiner Form ist der Zuschnitt aufwändiger als bei herkömmli-chen runden, drei- oder vier-eckigen Schildern, und es wird dabei mehr Material verbraucht. Auch wenn man sich auf die Form relativ rasch einigte, war es bis zum endgültigen Erschei-nungsbild des Schildes ein lan-ger Weg. Zuerst stand STOP in schwarzen Lettern auf weißem Grund, bald darauf in Schwarz auf Gelb, dann in Rot auf Gelb und endlich in der weltbekann-ten Endversion Weiß auf Rot. In den USA hat das Schild heute reflektierende Katzenaugen und ein Standardmaß von 76,2 x 76,2 cm, es sollte im Idealfall in 2,1 m Höhe installiert werden. Stoppschilder sieht man mitt-lerweile überall in der Welt. Während die spanischsprachi-gen Länder in Mittel- und Süda-merika noch immer das spani-sche Wort PARE oder ALTO be-nutzen, steht in Spanien auf den Schildern das englische STOP. Daran haben allerdings die Spa-nier keine Schuld – sie halten sich nur an die Richtlinien der Europäischen Union.

Ayant fait ses débuts aux États-Unis dès 1915, le STOP est au-jourd'hui le seul panneau de signa-lisation officiel à présenter partout, par convention internationale, une forme octogonale. S'il est unique en son genre, c'est autant par sou-ci d'économie que pour des rai-sons de sécurité : ses huit angles nécessitent en effet un temps de coupe plus long (et occasionnent plus de perte) que les carrés, tri-angles et cercles habituels. Si la dé-cision concernant l'adoption de l'octogone s'est faite assez rapi-dement, le choix du modèle a connu quelques flottements. On opta tout d'abord pour des carac-tères noirs sur fond blanc, puis on essaya le noir sur jaune, puis le rou-ge sur jaune, avant d'adopter défi-nitivement notre bon vieux blanc sur rouge. Aux États-Unis, il est à présent doté de réflecteurs de type catadioptres, mesure 76,2 x 76,2 cm et doit être installé à 2,1 m du sol. Et on le rencontre aux quatre coins du globe. Si, dans les États hispanophones d'Amé-rique latine, on y lit encore « PARE » ou « ALTO », l'Espagne elle-mê-me s'est mise au mot « STOP », à l'anglaise. Non par goût particulier pour la langue de Shakespeare : elle a simplement dû se conformer aux normes européennes.

41

43
Dog
Hund
Chien

Dog food
Hund in Dosen
Chien en boîte

A Dalmatian is dragged out of a cage and into the alley behind Chilsung market in Taegu, South Korea. As a rope tightens around its neck, the dog defecates from shock. A metal rod connected to an electric generator is shoved into its mouth, and electricity surges through its frame. The process is repeated several times. Stunned but not dead, its entire body is seared with a blowtorch to burn off the fur. The whole procedure lasts an hour. Its purpose is to make the dog secrete as much adrenaline as possible at the moment of death. The adrenaline-rich meat is believed to be a powerful aphrodisiac, giving men long-lasting erections. Most of the two million dogs eaten annually in South Korea are roasted or prepared as *youngyangtang* (healthy soup), and sold for 20,000 won (US$16) per kilogram. While the meat spoils quickly if not refrigerated, the erection, legend has it, can last for hours.

Taegu (Südkorea): Ein Dalmatiner wird aus dem Käfig gezerrt und in die Gasse hinter den Chilsung-Markt geschleift. Als sich die Schlinge um seinen Hals zuzieht, macht der Hund vor Schreck einen Haufen. Ein Metallstab, der mit einem Generator verbunden ist, wird ihm in die Schnauze gesteckt, und er bekommt einen kräftigen Stromstoß. Dieser Prozess wird ein paarmal wiederholt. Wenn der Hund benommen, aber noch nicht tot ist, wird ihm mit einem Gasbrenner am ganzen Körper das Fell abgesengt. Die gesamte Prozedur dauert etwa eine Stunde. Man will den Hund dazu bringen, im Moment seines Todes so viel Adrenalin wie möglich abzusondern, da adrenalinhaltiges Hundefleisch als Potenzmittel gilt, das Männern angeblich zu besonders lang anhaltenden Erektionen verhilft. Der Großteil der 2 Millionen Hunde, die jährlich in Südkorea auf den Tisch kommen, wird gebraten oder zu *youngyangtang* (Gesundheitssuppe) verarbeitet. Man bekommt Hundefleisch für 20 000 Won (24 US$) das Kilogramm. Während das Fleisch ungekühlt rasch verdirbt, können die Erektionen, so heißt es jedenfalls, stundenlang andauern.

Un dalmatien est extirpé de sa cage et traîné dans une allée, derrière le marché Chilsung, à Taegu (Corée du Sud). Étranglé à l'aide d'une corde, le chien défèque sous le choc. Une tige métallique reliée à un générateur est enfilée dans sa bouche, puis on lui envoie une série de décharges électriques. Assommé mais pas mort, l'animal est ensuite passé au chalumeau afin de lui calciner le poil et de le peler. Toute cette procédure dure une heure et vise à faire secréter au chien autant d'adrénaline que possible au moment de la mort. On vous expliquera qu'une viande riche en adrénaline est un puissant aphrodisiaque, garantie de très longues érections. Les 2 millions de chiens consommés annuellement en Corée du Sud sont pour la plupart rôtis ou préparés en *youngyangtang* (soupe de santé), puis vendus 20 000 WS (16 $ US) le kilo. La viande se gâte vite si elle n'est pas correctement réfrigérée, mais l'érection, à en croire la légende, durerait des heures entières.

BEWARE

OF
DOG

OUT

BOOF HEAD

BEWARE

MMG KILLERZ

THIS AREA IS PROTECTED BY
GUARD DOGS

BEWARE OF THE DOG

BHASOBHA INJA

ATTENTI AL CANE

E AL PADRONE

J'AIME
MON QUARTIER

JE RAMASSE

RÈGLEMENT SANITAIRE DÉPARTEMENTAL ART. 99-2
INFRACTION PUNIE PAR UNE AMENDE
POUVANT ATTEINDRE 3000F (457€)

IO NON POSSO ENTRARE

IO, DEVO
ESSERE TENUTO
AL GUINZAGLIO
E PORTARE LA
MUSERUOLA

POUSS

88

SPORTS AREA

DOGS
PROHIBITED

PER EVIDENTI RAGIONI
DI IGIENE
E' VIETATO INTRODURRE
ANIMALI
NEI LOCALI DI VENDITA

HUNDEVERBOT

55
Transport

Car blessing
Autosegen
Bénédiction de véhicule

At the Zenkoji Temple in Nagano, Japan, Buddhist priests specialize in blessing cars; the ¥5,000 (US$46) fee includes a wooden talisman to hang from the rearview mirror. Catholic priests sometimes formally bless cars, although a French bishop recently called for an end to this "hocuspocus." Kenya's taxi drivers just paint a prayer across their vehicle. "We are asking God to protect us from the hazards of our roads," says Robert Maina Kamanda, of Bombolulu (his taxi is decorated with "The Lord is my shepherd," in Swahili). "I feel safer because the Bible says, 'Ask and you shall receive.'"

Im Zenkoji-Tempel in Nagano (Japan) haben sich buddhistische Mönche darauf spezialisiert, Autos zu segnen (ein Segen kostet 5000 Yen oder 46 US$ einschließlich eines hölzernen Talismans, der an den Rückspiegel gehängt wird). Katholische Priester segnen ebenfalls hin und wieder Autos (auch wenn in Frankreich kürzlich ein Bischof empört forderte, diesem „Hokuspokus" ein Ende zu setzen). In Kenia malen Taxifahrer einfach Gebete auf ihre Fahrzeuge. „Wir bitten Gott um Schutz vor den Gefahren der Straße", erklärt Robert Maina Kamanda aus Bombulu (sein Taxi trägt die Aufschrift ‚Der Herr ist mein Hirte' in Suaheli). „So fühle ich mich sicherer, denn in der Bibel steht: ‚Bittet, dann wird euch gegeben.'"

Au temple Zenkoji de Nagano (Japon) officient quelques prêtres bouddhistes spécialistes de la bénédiction automobile (au tarif de 5000¥ [46 $US], avec talisman de bois à suspendre au rétroviseur fourni sans supplément). Il arrive aussi que des prêtres catholiques consacrent dans les règles un véhicule (bien qu'en France, un évêque ait récemment appelé à ce que cessent ces rituels «charlatanesques»). Les chauffeurs de taxi kenyans se contentent quant à eux de peindre une prière en travers de leur carrosserie. «Nous demandons à Dieu de nous protéger contre les dangers de nos routes», indique Robert Maina Kamanda, de Bombolulu (son taxi porte la mention «Le seigneur est mon berger» en swahili). «Comme ça, poursuit-il, je me sens plus en sécurité, car la Bible dit, "Demandez et il vous sera accordé".»

NEW SEAL

Breaking the rules
Gesetzesbrecher
Infractions

Only 12 out of every 1,000 Nigerians owns a car. This makes public transport a lucrative business. "The transport system here is controlled by gangs," says Seye Solola, a bus conductor in Lagos. The most terrible gangs are called *agbero* [touts] and they extort money from the drivers by force. The touts complain that they don't deserve their bad reputation: They're just doing their job. "As a 'motor parks official' I act as a tax collector," says Sulaimon Atere, 26. "I can't say that the tax we collect is legal or illegal. The touts are onetime drivers; since we are out of work, we must devise a way to earn a living. We have to be violent because drivers resist us when we approach them peaceably."

Lediglich zwölf von 1000 Nigerianern besitzen ein Auto. Das macht öffentliche Verkehrsmittel zum lukrativen Geschäft. „Das öf-

fentliche Verkehrssystem wird hierzulande von Banden beherrscht", erklärt Seye Solola, der in Lagos als Busfahrer arbeitet. Am schlimmsten seien die *Agbero* (Anreißer), die den Fahrern mit Gewalt Geld abpressten. Die Anreißer meinen, sie hätten ihren schlechten Ruf nicht verdient: Sie täten nur ihre Arbeit. „Als ‚Beamter des Wagenparks' muss ich Steuern eintreiben", meint Sulaimon Atere (26). „Ob die Steuern, die wir einziehen, dem Gesetz entsprechen oder nicht – das weiß ich nicht. Wir Anreißer sind ehemalige Fahrer, aber da wir arbeitslos sind, müssen wir uns halt irgendwie durchschlagen. Und Gewalt müssen wir anwenden, weil die Fahrer Widerstand leisten, wenn wir mit friedlichen Mitteln unserem Geschäft nachgehen."

Seuls douze Nigérians sur 1 000 possèdent une voiture, ce qui fait des transports publics une affai-

re fort juteuse. « Ici, les transports sont aux mains des gangs », se désole Seye Solola, chauffeur de bus à Lagos. Les plus terribles, ce sont les *agbero* [rabatteurs], qui extorquent de l'argent aux chauffeurs. Concert de protestations chez les rabatteurs en question qui disent ne pas mériter leur mauvaise réputation. Ils ne font que leur travail, assurent-ils. « En tant que "responsable des aires de stationnement", j'ai en quelque sorte le rôle d'un percepteur, explique Sulaimon Atere, 26 ans. Je ne pourrais pas dire si les taxes [de stationnement] que nous prélevons sont légales ou illégales. Tous les rabatteurs sont eux-mêmes d'anciens chauffeurs. Comme nous n'avons plus de travail, il faut bien trouver un moyen de gagner sa vie. Et on est obligés d'être violents parce que les chauffeurs nous résistent quand on les approche pacifiquement. »

ویگن سٹاپ

ملٹری پولیس

PARADA

Tired truckers
Übermüdete Trucker
Camionneurs épuisés

A third of fatal truck accidents are caused by fatigue (usually between 3am and 5am). So it's hardly surprising that staying awake is an obsession for most long-distance truckers. In Kenya many chew khat leaves, an illegal and addictive stimulant. Thai truck drivers prefer to smoke *ya maa*, a powerful amphetamine, even though possession of a single tablet can earn offenders a five-year prison sentence and a 50,000 baht (US$1,250) fine. Public safety, however, takes second place to the demands of the economy. "When I work I have to use it, otherwise I fall asleep," says Thon, 37, who drives trucks in northern Thailand during the sugarcane harvest, from December to March. He gets by on four to five hours of sleep a day. Though US regulations require truck drivers to sleep eight hours a day, the Thai authorities would rather not know. As Thon says, "The police wouldn't interfere, because the sugar is exported to foreign countries."

Ein Drittel aller tödlichen Lkw-Unfälle sind auf Übermüdung (die meist zwischen drei und fünf Uhr morgens auftritt) zurückzuführen. Von daher ist es verständlich, dass Wachbleiben für Langstrecken-Trucker zur fixen Idee werden kann. In Kenia kauen viele *khat*, ein illegales, Sucht erzeugendes Stimulans. Thailändische Fahrer verlassen sich auf *ya maa*, ein hochwirksames Amphetamin, auch wenn der Besitz einer einzigen Tablette mit fünf Jahren Haft und einer Geldbuße von 50 000 Baht (1250 US$) bestraft werden kann. Aber die öffentliche Sicherheit ist zweitrangig, wenn es um wirtschaftliche Interessen geht. „Wenn ich arbeite, muss ich das Zeug nehmen, sonst schlafe ich ein", erklärt Thon, 37, der während der Zuckerrohrernte von Dezember bis März in Nordthailand als Saisonarbeiter Lkw fährt. Er kommt mit vier bis fünf Stunden Schlaf aus. In den USA ist für Lkw-Fahrer eine tägliche Ruhezeit von acht Stunden vorgeschrieben, die thailändischen Behörden hingegen drücken oft beide Augen zu. Thon meint, die Polizei würde nicht eingreifen, weil der Zucker ins Ausland exportiert wird.

Un tiers des accidents de la route mortels impliquant des poids lourds sont imputables à la fatigue (la plupart surviennent entre trois et cinq heures du matin). Rien d'étonnant donc, si, pour les routiers effectuant de longs trajets, rester éveillé tourne à l'obsession. Au Kenya, beaucoup mâchent des feuilles de *qat*, un stimulant illégal entraînant une dépendance. Les camionneurs thaïlandais préfèrent fumer du *ya maa*, une puissante amphétamine, bien que la détention d'une tablette soit passible d'une peine de cinq ans et d'une amende de 50 000 BAHT (1 250 $ US). Cependant, les exigences économiques priment sur la sécurité publique. «Quand je travaille, je suis obligé d'en prendre, sinon je m'endors», confie Thon, 37 ans, qui transporte la canne à sucre dans le nord du pays en période de récolte (de décembre à mars). Et pour cause : il vit au régime de quatre à cinq heures de sommeil par nuit. Certes, la réglementation américaine exige des nuits de huit heures pour les chauffeurs routiers, mais les autorités thaïlandaises préfèrent l'ignorer. Comme dit Thon, « la police nous laisse faire, vu que le sucre est un produit d'exportation. »

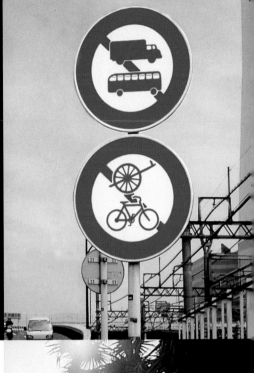

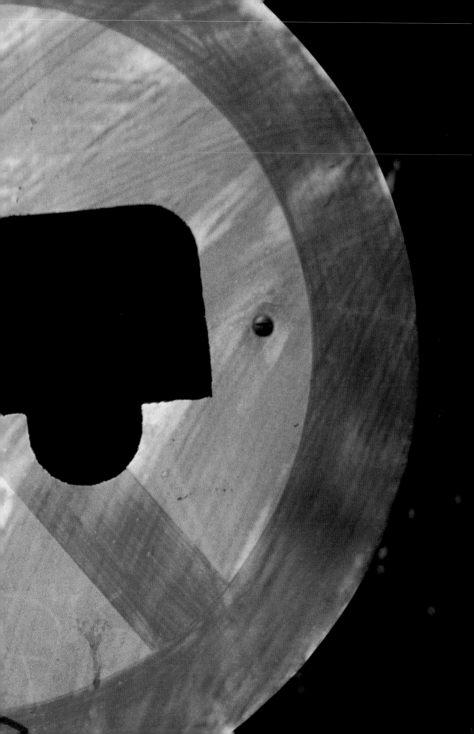

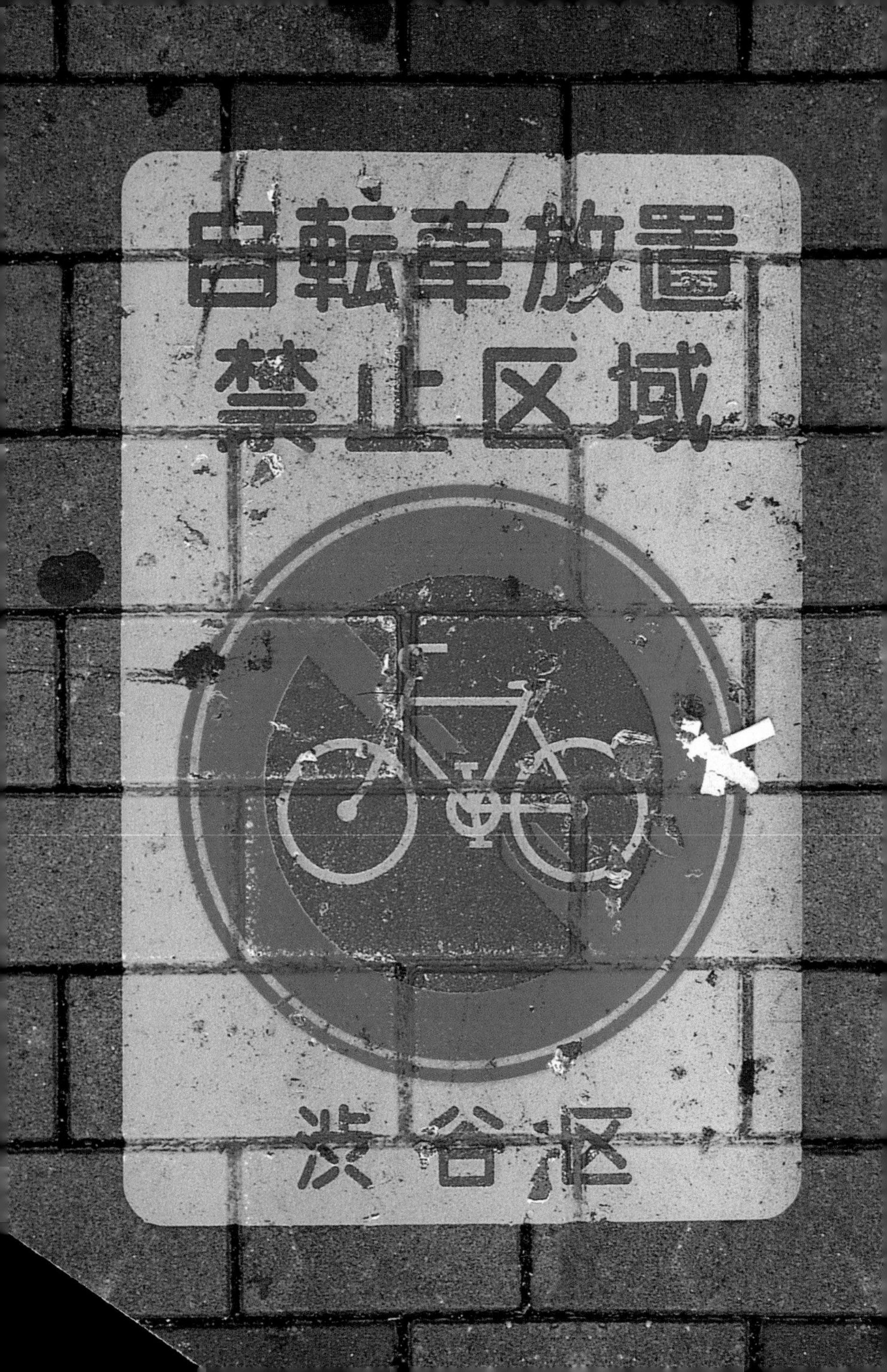
自転車放置
禁止区域
渋谷区

89
Children
Kinder
Enfants

SCHOOL

線路に物を落された方は
駅係員にお申し出ください

School lunch
Schulspeisung
Tous à la cantine !

Slips left in a school lunch suggestion box in Oakwood Friends School in Poughkeepsie, USA, called for more barbecued chicken wings, grilled cheese and french fries. During the 2001-2002 economic crisis in Argentina, schoolchildren were given fewer menu choices. The crisis, which sent the currency crashing and inflation rates soaring, meant that unknown numbers of families went hungry. "Many provinces decided to keep school lunchrooms open for weekends and over the summer," Mariano Mohadeb, a spokesman for the Argentine Ministry of Education, said at the time, "because so many kids are going to school not only to study but also to eat. It's the only place they can get food." The Ministry freed up 5 million pesos (US$1.7 million) to pay for the school feeding program in 10 provinces, believing it would help around 800,000 children in 6,000 schools. "Schools have always played an enormous role in society," said Mohadeb. "In this time of crisis, they are playing a bigger role than ever."

An der Oakwood-Friends-Schule in Poughkeepsie (USA) hätten die Schüler – wie aus ihren Wunschzetteln für die Schulspeisung hervorgeht – zum Mittagessen gern mehr Barbecue-Hühnerflügel, gegrillten Käse und Pommes frites. In Argentinien hatten die Schülerinnen und Schüler während der Wirtschaftskrise 2001-2002 weniger Auswahl. Die Krise, die die Währung ins Bodenlose fallen ließ, während die Inflation himmelhoch stieg, führte dazu, dass zahlreiche argentinische Familien Hunger litten. „In vielen Provinzen blieben die Schulkantinen auch an Wochenenden und in den Sommerferien geöffnet", erklärte Mariano Mohadeb vom argentinischen Kultusministerium, „weil viele Kinder nicht nur zum Lernen in die Schule gehen, sondern auch zum Essen. Nur dort bekommen sie eine warme Mahlzeit." Das Ministerium stellte für das Schulspeisungsprogramm in zehn Provinzen 5 Millionen Pesos (1,7 Millionen US$) zur Verfügung, um damit schätzungsweise 800 000 Kindern in 6000 Schulen zu helfen. „Schulen spielen seit jeher eine bedeutende Rolle in der Gesellschaft", meint Mariano. „In der gegenwärtigen Krisensituation sind sie wichtiger denn je."

Les petits mots glissés dans la boîte à idées «cantine» de l'école Oakwood Friends de Poughkeepsie (États-Unis) réclamaient invariablement plus de poulet au barbecue, plus de fromage grillé ou plus de frites. Durant la crise économique que traversa l'Argentine en 2001–2002, les écoliers n'avaient pas autant de choix au menu. Avec une monnaie au plus bas et une inflation galopante, la faim était devenue une réalité quotidienne pour un nombre important – et indéterminé – de familles. «De nombreuses provinces ont décidé de maintenir les cantines des écoles ouvertes les weekends et pendant l'été, nous signalait à l'époque Mariano Mohadeb, du ministère argentin de l'Éducation, parce que beaucoup d'enfants à présent vont à l'école non seulement pour s'instruire, mais aussi pour manger. C'est le seul endroit où ils sont assurés d'être nourris.» Ledit ministère avait débloqué 5 millions de pesos (1,7 million $ US) afin de financer dans 10 provinces ces repas de cantine, escomptant secourir ainsi 800 000 enfants dans 6 000 établissements scolaires. «L'école a toujours joué un rôle capital dans la société, soulignait Mariano. En ce temps de crise, sa mission est plus importante que jamais.»

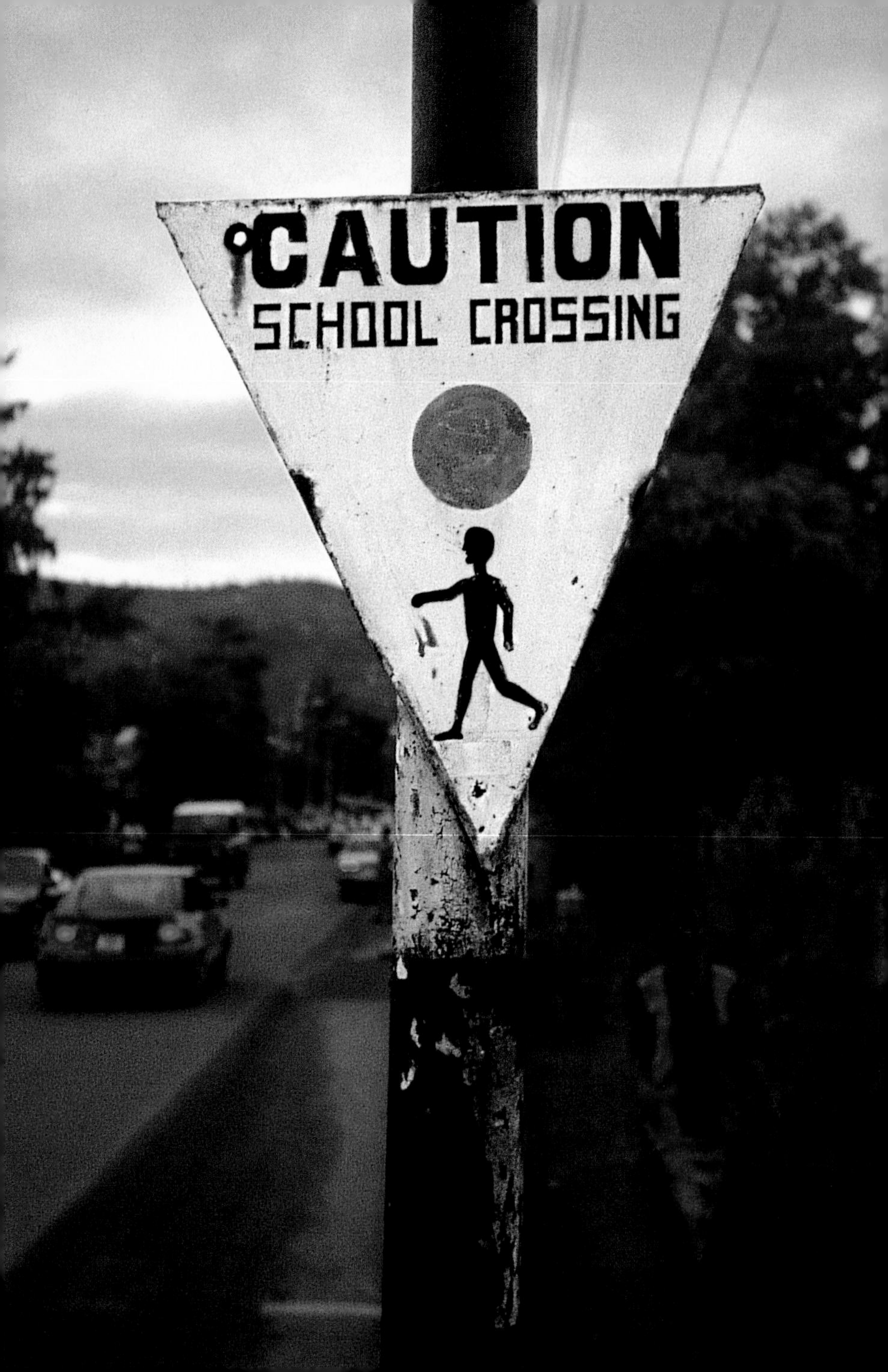
CAUTION
SCHOOL CROSSING

School
學校

Skole

111
Miscellaneous
Verschiedenes
En vrac

WELCOME
TO
MOON LAND

MOREPLAN

ENJOY NATURE

WHILE DRIVING

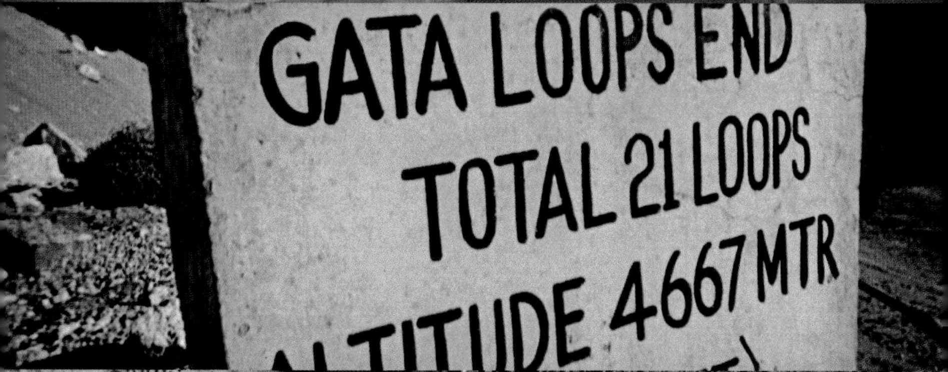

GATA LOOPS END
TOTAL 21 LOOPS
ALTITUDE 4667 MTR

BORDER ROADS ORGANISATION

-AST WON'T LAST

GREF

81

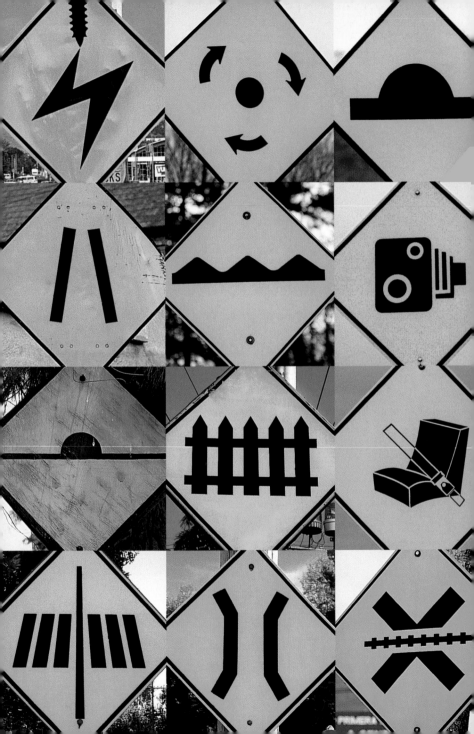

123
Danger
Gefahr
Danger

Last meal
Letzte Mahlzeit
Dernier repas

At 4.30pm on May 30, 2002, Stanley Allison Baker Jr. began eating two 500g rib eye steaks, 450g of thinly sliced turkey, 12 rashers of bacon, two hamburgers with mayonnaise, onion and lettuce, two large baked potatoes with butter, sour cream, cheese and chives, four slices of cheese, a chef salad with blue-cheese dressing, two ears of corn, and one tub of mint chocolate chip ice cream. He drank four vanilla Coca-Colas. At 5:55 pm Baker was taken from his cell on death row at the Polunsky Unit in Livingston, Texas, USA, to the death chamber in Huntsville Prison, where he was executed by lethal injection—a chemical cocktail of sodium thiopental (to sedate), pancuronium bromide (to collapse the diaphragm and lungs), and potassium chloride (to stop the heart).

The prison in Huntsville has the busiest death chamber in the USA. By November 2002, 31 people had been executed there—over half of the executions in the country. Prosecuting Baker cost the state of Texas around US$2.16 million over and above the cost of a trial that does not involve the death penalty (or about three times the cost of imprisoning someone in a single cell at the highest security level for 40 years).

Death penalty trials last longer and, because sentences are almost automatically appealed, prisoners remain on death row for an average of 10 years and 7 months. Cutting the right to appeal would be a money-saving measure, but the price could be high: A 2000 Columbia University Law School study found that 68 percent of death penalty verdicts appealed between 1973 and 1995 were so seriously flawed that they had to be sent back for a new trial or resentencing.

Am 30. Mai 2002 um 16.30 Uhr begann Stanley Allison Baker jr. mit dem Verzehr von zwei 500 g schweren Ribeye-Steaks, 450 g Puter in feinen Scheiben, zwölf Scheiben gebratenem Speck, zwei Hamburgern mit Mayonnaise, Zwiebelringen und Salat, zwei dicken Ofenkartoffeln mit Butter, Sour Cream, Käse und Schnittlauch, vier Scheiben Käse, einem Chef-Salat mit Blauschimmelkäse-Dressing, zwei Maiskolben und einer Familienpackung Pfefferminzeis mit Schokosplittern. Dazu trank er vier Dosen Cola mit Vanillegeschmack. Um 17.55 Uhr wurde Stanley aus seiner Zelle im Todestrakt der Polunsky Unit in Livingston (Texas) in die Exekutionskammer im Gefängnis von

Huntsville gebracht, wo er per Todesspritze hingerichtet wurde – mittels eines Chemikaliencocktails aus Natriumpenthotal (zur Beruhigung), Pancuroniumbromid (zur Lähmung der Atmungsorgane) und Potassiumchlorid (das zum Herzstillstand führt).

In der Hinrichtungszelle von Huntsville ist viel los. Dort finden die meisten Exekutionen der USA statt: Bis November 2002 wurden dort 31 Todesurteile vollstreckt, über die Hälfte des ganzen Landes. Stanleys Strafverfolgung kostete den Staat Texas schätzungsweise 2,16 Millionen US$ mehr als ein Gerichtsverfahren bei dem nicht die Todesstrafe auf dem Spiel steht, oder dreimal so viel wie eine 40-jährige Haftstrafe in einer Einzelzelle im Hochsicherheitstrakt. Prozesse, bei denen das Todesurteil verhängt wird, dauern länger, weil beinahe automatisch Berufung eingelegt wird und der Verurteilte durchschnittlich zehn Jahre und sieben Monate in der Todeszelle sitzt. Das Recht auf Berufung abzuschaffen würde selbstverständlich die Kosten senken, doch um welchen Preis? Eine Studie der juristischen Fakultät der Columbia University aus dem Jahr 2000 hat nachgewiesen, dass 68% alle Urteile, bei denen die Todesstra-

fe verhängt wurde und die zwischen 1973 und 1995 in die Berufung gingen, so fehlerhaft waren, dass der gesamte Prozess wieder augerollt oder das Urteil neu formuliert werden musste.

Le 30 mai 2002, à 16h30, Stanley Allison Baker Jr entama un repas composé comme suit : deux entrecôtes de 500 g, 450 g d'émincé de dinde, 12 tranches de bacon, deux hamburgers avec mayonnaise, oignon et laitue, deux grosses pommes de terre au four accompagnées de beurre, de crème aigre, de fromage et de ciboulette, quatre tranches de fromage, une salade du chef avec une vinaigrette au bleu, deux épis de maïs et un petit pot de crème glacée à la menthe et aux pépites de chocolat. Le tout arrosé de quatre Coca-Colas goût vanille. À 17h55, on sortit Stanley de sa cellule, dans le couloir de la mort de la division carcérale de Polunsky, à Livingston, Texas (États-Unis), pour le conduire dans la « chambre de la mort » de la prison de Huntsville, où il fut exécuté par injection létale – un cocktail de trois substances chimiques, le thiopental de sodium (un sédatif), le bromure de pancuronium (qui inhibe le diaphragme et les poumons) et le chlorure de potassium (qui provoque un arrêt cardiaque).

De toutes les salles d'exécution du pays, celle de la prison de Huntsville est de loin la plus active. En novembre 2002, on y avait procédé à 31 mises à mort, soit plus de la moitié de celles pratiquées sur l'ensemble du pays. Comparé à un procès n'impliquant pas la peine capitale, condamner Stanley à mort a généré pour l'État du Texas un surcoût de procédure d'environ 2,16 millions $ US (soit trois fois le coût de 40 ans d'incarcération en cellule individuelle dans un quartier de très haute sécurité). En effet, les procès des condamnés à mort durent plus longtemps et, la défense faisant presque systématiquement appel, les séjours des détenus dans les couloirs de la mort s'éternisent (leur durée moyenne est de dix ans et sept mois). Pour réduire les frais, d'aucuns seraient tentés de supprimer le droit d'appel, mais le prix à payer risque d'être plus élevé encore. En effet, une étude menée en 2000 par la faculté de droit de l'université de Columbia a révélé que 68 % des peines capitales réexaminées en appel entre 1973 et 1995 recouvraient de tels vices de procédure que les tribunaux devaient être re-convoqués, soit pour entamer un nouveau procès, soit pour revoir les verdicts.

ब्लॉक 140
मकान 1243 से 1256

WARNING
THIS BLDG HAS BEEN NOTIFIED AS DANGEROUS
ALL TRESSPASSERS ARE HEREBY WARNED
TO KEEP AWAY FROM THIS BLDG -
AND RESPONSIBILITY FOR LOSS OF LIFE AND
PROPERTY LIES WITH THE DEFAULTERS
BY ORDER
EXECUTIVE ENGINEER/MCD II /MUMBAI 37

KABI
DANGER
HATARI
ಐ ऊ,।ᵃ
UGANDA ELECTRICITY BOARD

DANGER

S
4

T
8

አደገኛ

R

246

CARICO E S

NON TOCCATE I FILI

PERICOLO DI MORTE

ALTA

TENSION

YÜKSEK
VOLTAJ

GAS INFIAMMABILI

**POZOR!
VISOKA NAPETOST
SMRTNO NEVARNO**

**CAUTION
FORK LIFT
TRUCKS IN
OPERATION**

DANGE

Opening

in floo

Nevarnost
eksplozije !

Underground
Unterirdisch
Sous-sol

The Australian town of Coober Pedy is known as the "Opal Capital of the World." It's also known for low census returns, low voter turnout, high tax avoidance, gambling, and drinking. Many of its 4,000 residents—who mine 70 percent of the world's opals—live in cave dwellings to escape the year-round intense outback heat. There are underground hotels and churches too, dug out by World War I soldiers on their return from the trenches. Forty-five nationalities work in the mines, though one is missing: Australian aborigines, who though they discovered the largest seam of gems in 1946, have been frozen out of the bonanza, and are mostly found begging on the streets. They call the town *kupa piti*, or "white man's hole in the ground."

Die australische Stadt Coober Pedy ist allgemein als „Welthauptstadt des Opals" bekannt, aber auch für das geringe Interesse ihrer Einwohner an Volkzählungen und Wahlen, für Steuerhinterziehung, Glücksspiel und Alkoholkonsum. Viele der 4000 Einwohner, die 70% aller Opale der Welt schürfen, leben in unterirdischen Wohnungen, um der ganzjährigen drückenden Hitze des australischen Hinterlandes zu entkommen. Es gibt auch unterirdische Hotels und Kirchen, die von Soldaten nach ihrer Rückkehr aus den Schützengräben des Ersten Weltkriegs angelegt wurden. In den Bergwerken arbeiten Menschen, die 45 verschiedenen Nationalitäten angehören, wobei eine fehlt: Die australischen Aborigines, die 1946 die größte Opalader entdeckten, sind vom Abbau ausgeschlossen und ziehen größtenteils bettelnd durch die Straßen. Sie nennen die Stadt *kupa piti*, „Erdloch des weißen Mannes".

La ville australienne de Coober Pedy est connue comme la «capitale mondiale de l'opale». Elle a en outre acquis un certain renom pour la vie infernale qu'elle mène aux recenseurs, pour son taux d'abstention record aux suffrages électoraux, pour ses nombreux adeptes de l'évasion fiscale et pour sa population débauchée, qui s'adonne sans retenue au jeu et à l'alcool. Parmi ses 4000 habitants (qui extraient du sol 70% des opales du monde), beaucoup se terrent dans des habitations troglodytes afin d'échapper à la chaleur intense qui écrase l'intérieur du territoire australien. Il existe même des églises et des hôtels souterrains, construits par des poilus de la Grande Guerre à leur retour des tranchées. Parmi les 45 nationalités qui se côtoient dans les mines, il en est une dont l'absence se remarque: les aborigènes australiens, à qui l'on doit pourtant la découverte du plus gros filon de gemmes, en 1946, ont été écartés de cette manne prolifique, et on les retrouve désormais mendiant dans les rues de la ville. Du reste, ils nomment cette dernière *kupa piti*, ce qui signifie «trou d'homme blanc dans le sol».

Halkrisk

BEWARE OF SHALLOW WATER WHEN DIVING

147
Toilets
Toiletten
Toilettes

Untouchable
Unberührbare
Intouchables

Out of 1 billion people living in India, 700 million have no decent toilet. Men defecate wherever and whenever; women are forced, out of modesty, into dark fields before dawn and after sunset. In hygiene terms, India is a massive, open-air latrine, with health consequences to match (a child dies every eight seconds from sanitation-related diseases). To clean it up, there are the scavengers, people from India's lowest castes (Bhangi or Dalit), known more commonly as "untouchables." They probably originated from prisoners of war centuries ago, at the time of the Muslim invasions. Enlisted to clean up after *purdah* women who couldn't leave their quarters, untouchables emptied "night-soil" with their bare hands, and have yet to recover from the stigma. Hence their polluted status and a job that was never likely to be surplus to requirements. India has 135 million kg of excrement to dispose of every day, and over 600,000 people still make a living from night-soil removal.

Von einer Milliarde Indern haben 700 Millionen keinen Zugang zu sanitären Anlagen. Männer erledigen ihr großes Geschäft, wo und wann immer sie müssen, Frauen setzen sich aus Scham vor Sonnenaufgang und am späten Abend in dunkle Ecken und auf die Felder. Was die hygienischen Bedingungen angeht, ist Indien eine einzige riesige Freiluftlatrine – mit unsäglichen gesundheitlichen Folgen (alle acht Sekunden stirbt ein Kind an einer Krankheit, die mit mangelnder Hygiene zu tun hat). Den Dreck zu beseitigen ist die Aufgabe der Müllsammler, in der Regel Angehörige der niedrigsten Kasten in Indien, der Bhangi oder Dalit, die besser als „Unberührbare" bekannt sind. Diese Kategorie geht wahrscheinlich auf die Kriegsgefangenen zurück, die vor Jahrhunderten während der muslimischen Eroberungszüge dazu abkommandiert wurden, hinter den Haremsdamen „aufzuräumen", die ihre Gemächer nicht verlassen durften. Dazu gehörte auch, mit bloßen Händen ihren „nächtlichen Schmutz" zu entsorgen. Dieses Stigma hängt den Unberührbaren Jahrhunderte später noch an, ist der Grund für ihren Ausschluss aus der Gesellschaft und ihre undankbare Arbeit, die kaum jemals mehr als das Nötigste brachte: Tag für Tag sind in Indien 135 Millionen kg Exkremente zu beseitigen. Über 600 000 Menschen verdienen ihren Lebensunterhalt noch heute mit dem Wegschaffen nächtlichen Schmutzes.

Sur le milliard d'habitants que compte l'Inde, 700 millions ne disposent pas de toilettes dignes de ce nom. Les hommes défèquent n'importe où et n'importe quand, tandis que la pudeur oblige ces dames à filer à travers champs, dans l'obscurité du petit matin ou du crépuscule. En termes d'hygiène, le sous-continent indien est donc un gigantesque W.-C. à ciel ouvert, avec les retombées sanitaires que l'on imagine (un enfant meurt toutes les huit secondes d'une maladie directement liée au manque d'hygiène). Pour nettoyer ces toilettes géantes, la société indienne a ses volontaires désignés d'office, ses éboueurs de naissance. Il s'agit des membres des castes inférieures (*bhangi* et *dalit*), communément nommés les «intouchables» et descendants probables des prisonniers de guerre faits à l'époque des invasions musulmanes. Recrutés alors pour nettoyer les appartements des femmes cloîtrées au sérail, ils devaient vider leurs pots de chambre à la main. Aux yeux des autres castes, la souillure demeure et leurs doigts sont impurs à jamais. D'où leur statut d'individus «pollués» et l'emploi qu'on leur assigne – emploi pour lequel, au demeurant, l'offre ne risque jamais d'excéder la demande : l'Inde produit en effet (et doit par conséquent gérer) 135 millions de kilos d'excréments par jour. Plus de 600 000 personnes gagnent encore leur vie en ramassant les déjections nocturnes.

สุขาชาย

สุขาหญิง

पशु-पक्षां सारखी
घाण करु नका.
माणसा सारखे
जबाबदारीने वागा
आपला परिसर स्वच्छ
ठेवणे जरुरीचे आहे.

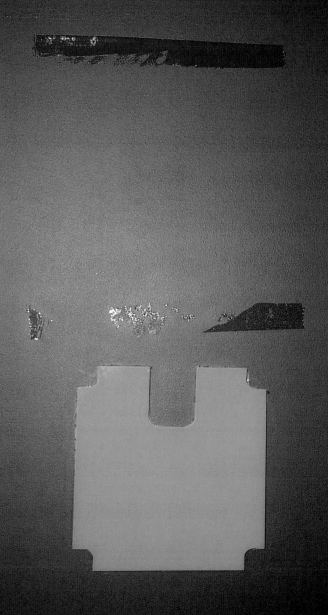

حمام الرجال

BAIN POUR HOMMES

WC

WC

BAIN POUR FEMMES

159

161
No!
Nein!
Non!

Please switch

不准擺賣

ETATO FUMARE

NS OR ARCHERY **NO ENTRY** ห้ามหาบเร่

NO SCOOTERS

ห้ามวัตถุไวไฟ

MODEL AEROPLANES

WARNING

DON'T LITTER

PLEASE!

DEPARTMENT OF SANITATION

NOTICE

NO BALL PLAYING.
NO CARRIAGES.
NO PEDDLING.
NO LOITERING.
NO SITTING IN FRONT OF
BUILDING ALLOWED.

O ENTRY

嚴禁進入

RYODEN LIFT & ESCALATOR

菱電升降機有限

NOTICE

**VIETATO
L'ACCESSO**

ห้ามเข้า   No Ent

Islet

CENTRAL
BEACH

CAUTION
Swimmers/children are
advised to swim within
the Rope-in-area

זהירות
עובדים
בדרך

179
Work
Arbeit
Travail

Men at work
Arbeiter
Chantier en cours

The future of humankind is underground. Subterranean real estate is inexpensive, weatherproof, energy-efficient and insulated from the sun's harmful rays. Stockholm, which already has an underground concert hall, plans subterranean pedestrian paths by the end of the century. With Tokyo bursting at the seams, Japan's gigantic Tokyu construction company has unveiled designs for an underground city, Geotropolis, to be habitable by the year 2020. And dozens of countries, including Scotland and Northern Ireland, are making plans to hook up by underwater tunnels.

Subterranean construction will mean lots of new jobs for people with the right skills. To learn how to operate the most advanced tunneling equipment (gigantic digging machines that bore up to 3.3cm of tunnel per minute), look for work in one of the many subways now in progress worldwide (London, Paris, Cairo, Lisbon, Toronto, Brasilia and Rome all have projects under way). As Rafik Karaouzen, a tunneler in the Cairo subway, told us, a prospective tunneler "should not be scared of working in tight, hot, closed-in places, nor mind getting dirty." Salaries are good in comparison with most construction

jobs, but beware of the risks: The high atmospheric pressure in tunnels (a result of air pumped in to prevent leakage) can lead to bone disease and lung trouble; carbon monoxide frequently reaches danger levels; and tunnel construction generally leaves one person dead every 1.6 kms.

Die Zukunft der Menschheit liegt unter der Erde. Unterirdische Immobilien sind billig, wetterfest, energiesparend und keinen schädlichen Sonnenstrahlen ausgesetzt. In Stockholm, das schon heute einen unterirdischen Konzertsaal hat, ist geplant, bis zum Ende des Jahrhunderts Fußgängerzonen unter Tage einzurichten. Für das überfüllte Tokio hat die Großbaufirma Tokyu Entwürfe für eine Untergrundstadt, Geotropolis, vorgelegt, die spätestens im Jahr 2020 beziehbar sein soll. Und in Dutzenden anderer Länder, darunter Schottland und Nordirland, werden Pläne für Unterwasser-Tunnelverbindungen geschmiedet.

Auf Baustellen unter Tage gibt es für Leute mit den richtigen Qualifikationen jede Menge Arbeitsplätze. Wenn ihr lernen wollt, wie man mit den modernsten Tunnelvortriebsmaschinen (riesigen Bohrern, die pro Minu-

te bis zu 3,3 cm Erde aushöhlen) umgeht, bewerbt euch auf einer der vielen U-Bahn-Baustellen der Welt (London, Paris, Kairo, Lissabon, Toronto, Brasilia und Rom erweitern zurzeit das Tunnelnetz). Rafik Karaouzen von der Kairoer U-Bahn meint, ein zukünftiger Tunnelgräber dürfe „nicht davor zurückschrecken, an engen, heißen, schwer zugänglichen Orten zu arbeiten und vor allem sich schmutzig zu machen". Das Lohnniveau liegt im Vergleich zu anderen Großbaustellen relativ hoch, dasselbe gilt aber für das Berufsrisiko: Der hohe Luftdruck in Tunneln (der auf die zugepumpte Luft, die Erdgeriesel verhindern soll, zurückzuführen ist) kann zu Knochenschäden und Lungenbeschwerden führen. Kohlenmonoxid erreicht oft bedenkliche Werte, und im Schnitt bleibt beim Tunnelbau alle 1,6 km wortwörtlich ein Arbeiter auf der Strecke.

L'avenir de l'homme est sous la terre. Songez plutôt : l'immobilier souterrain est peu coûteux, résistant aux intempéries, facile à chauffer et protégé des rayons nocifs du soleil. Stockholm, qui dispose déjà d'une salle de concert souterraine, projette de creuser des rues piétonnes sous

terre. Pour désengorger Tokyo, si surpeuplée qu'elle semble proche du point de rupture, l'énorme entreprise japonaise de BTP Tokyu a dévoilé les plans d'une cité souterraine, Geotropolis, qui serait habitable aux alentours de 2020. Des dizaines d'autres pays, notamment l'Écosse et l'Ulster, se lancent dans des projets de liaison par tunnel sous-marin.

Le domaine de la construction souterraine générera une manne de nouveaux emplois – pour ceux, bien entendu, qui présenteront les aptitudes requises. Alors, n'hésitez plus : initiez-vous dès à présent au fonctionnement des tunneliers les plus modernes et performants (ces gigantesques machines qui forent jusqu'à 3,3 cm de tunnel à la minute) en décrochant un emploi dans l'un des nombreux métros en chantier dans le monde (les villes de Londres, Paris, Le Caire, Lisbonne, Toronto, Brasilia et Rome ont toutes des projets en cours). Comme nous l'a expliqué Rafik Karaouzen, tunnelier dans le métro du Caire, un futur tunnelier « ne doit pas avoir peur du manque d'espace et des endroits confinés, ni craindre la chaleur et la saleté. » Les salaires sont avantageux, comparés à ceux habituellement pratiqués dans le BTP, mais attention aux risques : la forte pression atmosphérique qui règne dans les tunnels (en raison de l'air pulsé que l'on y introduit afin d'éviter les fuites) peut provoquer des maladies osseuses et des troubles respiratoires ; le monoxyde de carbone y atteint souvent des niveaux de concentration dangereux ; enfin, la construction des tunnels fait en moyenne un mort tous les 1,6 km.

VIETATO L'ACCESSO AI NON ADDETTI

VSTOP NEZAPOSLENIM PREPOVEDAN

Förbjudet fö obehöriga at beträd

SOLO PERSONAL
AUTORIZADO

ALLUR AKSTUR
'BANNAÐUR'
- NEMA LÖGREGLA OG SLÖKKVILIÐ

Page/Country/Photographer
Page/Pays/Photographe
Seite/Land/Fotograf

SIGNS is a project by COLORS Magazine

To stay informed about upcoming TASCHEN titles, please
request our magazine at www.taschen.com/magazine or write to
TASCHEN, Hohenzollernring 53, D-50672 Cologne, Germany,
contact@taschen.com, Fax: +49-221-254919. We will be happy to send
you a free copy of our magazine which is filled with information about all
of our books.

Editors Carlos Mustienes and Thomas Hilland
Art director Marco Callegari
Co editor Giuliana Rando
Associate editors Samantha Bartoletti and Grégoire Basdevant
Editorial coordination Thierry Nebois
Text editor Tom Ridgway
German editor Karen Gerhards
French editor Isabelle Baraton

Editorial director Renzo di Renzo

Production Marco Callegari
Lithography Sartori Group S.r.l.
Thank you Bruno Ceschel, Giovanna Dunmall, Sara Gaiotto,
Rose George, Michele Lunardi, Michael Medelin,
Loris Pasetto, Renzo Saccaro, Claudio Sartori,
Janine Stephen, Suzanne Wales, Fiona Wilson.

Printed in Italy
ISBN 978–3–8228–4839–5

Graphic Design for the 21ˢᵗ Century
Eds. Charlotte & Peter Fiell / Flexi-cover, 192 pp. / € 6.99 / $ 9.99 / £ 5.99 / ¥ 1.500

Design of the 20ᵗʰ Century
Eds. Charlotte & Peter Fiell / Flexi-cover, 192 pp. / € 6.99 / $ 9.99 / £ 5.99 / ¥ 1.500

Design for the 21ᵗʰ Century
Eds. Charlotte & Peter Fiell / Flexi-cover, 192 pp. / € 6.99 / $ 9.99 / £ 5.99 / ¥ 1.500

"These books are beautiful objects, well-designed and lucid." —*Le Monde*, Paris, on the ICONS series

" Buy them all and add some pleasure to your life."